MOONLIGHT

A RISE OF THE SUMMER GOD ADVENTURE

VOLUME I

Summer H Hanford

A Battle of Gods and Kingdoms

SUMMER HANFORD

This is a work of fiction. Names, characters, businesses, places, events, locales, and incidents are products of the author's imagination. Any resemblance to reality is coincidental.

ISBN: 979-8-3401158-9-8

www.summerhanford.com

MORE BY SUMMER HANFORD

Rise of the Summer God Series
Daughters of Awen
Battle of Greypass
Wyvern's Call
Shroud of Fate
Shards of Deceit
Destiny of Truth

Thrice Born Series
Gift of the Aluien
Hawks of Sorga
Throne of Wheylia
The Plains of Tybrunn
Shores of K'Orge
Thrice Born Chronicles

Crown & Dagger Swashbuckling Tales
Kestrel
Red Fox
Forest Hart

Pride & Prejudice and Planets:
An Alternate-Reality Pride & Prejudice Science Fiction
Variation

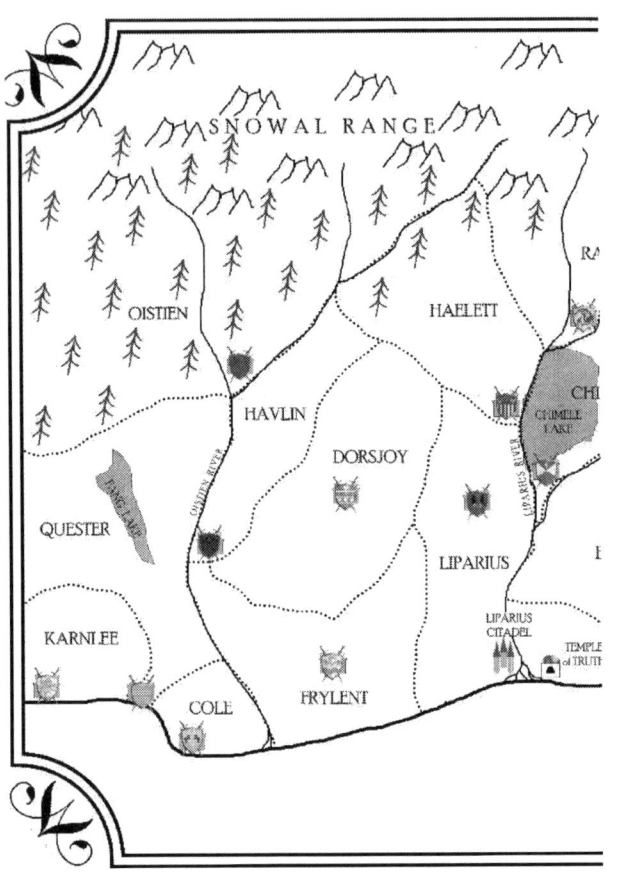

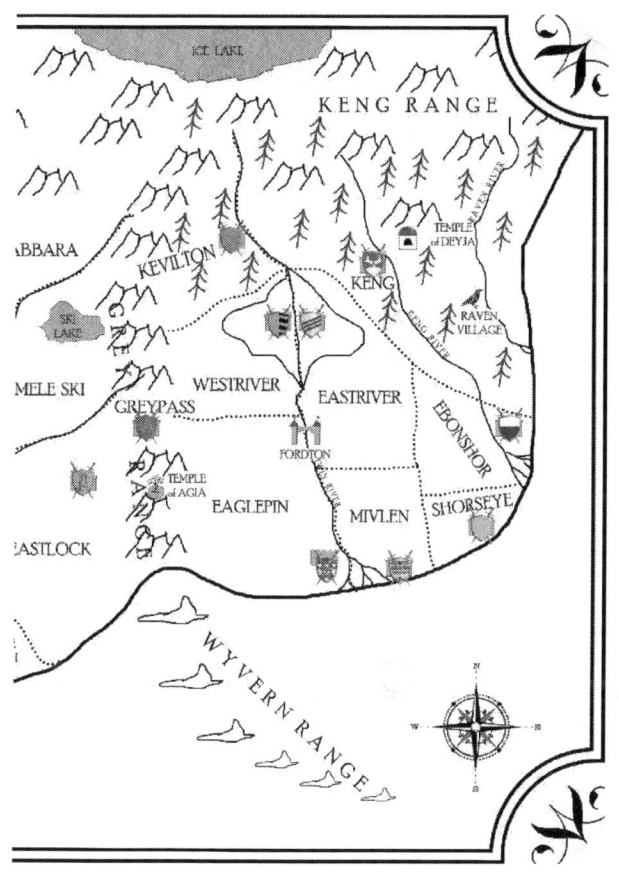

TRIAL BY MOONLIGHT

I

Nestled in bed in the small domed hut she shared in the raven village, Aldera dreamed of her home to the west. Of the fields, hills, and valleys where she once lived, soon to burgeon with the glory of spring. Of her mother rising early to bake hearty brown bread and her father readying the team to till the rich earth. And of her younger brother, Kylem, wielding his wooden sword as he pretended to be a knight. Would he have grown in the months she'd been here? She hadn't seen him since autumn, when she'd fled her home and come to live with her mother's people.

A hand settled on Aldera's shoulder. Panic surged through her. She threw off the thick quilt and sat up.

Blinking, she took in a ring of oval faces framed in dark locks, all bathed in the flickering yellow glow of candlelight. Each of the other girls, ranging from her hut-mate Pana's age of nine to a little older than Aldera, held a lit stub. The rich scent of the berries from which they rendered the wax and the herbs they added when they melted it down washed over Aldera, calming.

Pana released her shoulder with a grimace. "You do not need to act as if we're accosting you. You are always so uneasy."

Aldera had no answer to that, for even after half

a year of living and studying in the pinewood with the women and girls there, she was unaccustomed to living among those the rest of the kingdom of Cendoria labeled as witches. "Why did you wake me? Is something amiss?" The faces about her ranged from grave to eager, the disparity adding to her confusion.

"That depends on you," Pana said cryptically. "Get dressed. We will be waiting outside."

Aldera shook her head, her own dark locks tumbling about her. "Is it not the middle of the night?"

In the act of turning away, Pana halted. "It is just past midnight. It is your twelfth birthday."

Aldera watched them leave, wondering what her birthday had to do with anything. Under Pana's reluctant guidance, Aldera had been studying the customs of her mother's people for months and knew of a ritual that took place the sixteenth year after her birth, but had learned nothing of the twelfth.

Uneasy, for Pana was not above tormenting her for any ignorance, Aldera dressed in the gray trousers and tunic of the raven women. She quickly plaited her hair as well, the waist-length black locks prone to getting in her way. On her way out of the hut, she snatched her long gray cloak from its peg near the door, for winter had not yet released the land from an icy grasp.

The other girls waited, most of their candles extinguished. In the cleared space of the village, if the raven women's collection of huts and their mounded, earthen temple could truly be called such, the waning winter moon provided enough light by which to see. Even more than they had by candlelight, the moon-bleached forms that gathered about Aldera were wraithlike and daunting.

But Aldera wouldn't give Pana the satisfaction of seeing her fear. She fastened her cloak and strode into the heart of the semicircle of girls. Whispering, for other huts were near, she asked, "What are we doing?" *More importantly, did the women of the village know they were doing it?*

"Today the sun will rise on your twelfth year." Though quiet as well, Pana's voice held the singsong quality it always took on when she repeated something she'd learned by rote. "Before it does, you must pass our trials or you will never be accepted by our goddess. You must prove your bravery to be worthy of the Raven Goddess of Winter's love."

Aldera pressed her lips together, thinking. "What trials? I haven't read about them. You haven't taught me about them, either."

Pana leveled a derisive, disappointed look on Aldera, combining both her disgust in her new sister's ignorance with pity for her upbringing. "It is not my fault you don't know anything."

"You are the one Saderia set to teach me," Aldera cast back, referencing the only power Pana seemed to recognize outside the mysterious Raven Goddess of Winter. That of the leader of the village, their Saderia, Pana's mother.

"Yes, but you learn so slow. We've been practicing since autumn and you still speak our language like a baby." Pana huffed and added, "A tiny, helpless baby."

"You truly do have to go through the trials, Aldera," one of the other girls, Talla, said. "I did last year. We all do."

Reassured, for Talla was far more reliable than Pana, Aldera nodded. "What must I do?"

"There are three trials." Pana spoke eagerly now. "The first lies there." Her eyes bright with glee even by moonlight, she pointed to the center of the village, where a hillock stood. Tree-topped and squat, the hill held a single door. That door led into the first room of the temple, where the books of knowledge were kept.

And where Crawa, guardian of secrets and of the ravens, lurked.

Aldera swallowed a hard lump of fear. "In the temple?"

The girls about her nodded.

"You must enter and not return until you hold the feather of a raven," Pana said. "If you are worthy, the birds will grant you one." Her gaze flicked to Talla. "Talla came out with a tail feather but when I come out, it will be with a wing feather. Maybe even two."

"Some girls come back with down," one of the others whispered, her tone derisive.

Aldera hardly heard the words, her attention on the dark doorway that led into Crawa's realm. The ancient, gaunt keeper of the ravens answered only to Saderia and rarely spoke to anyone else. She did not join the other women in gathering reeds or berries, or making candles or cloth. Stooped, with jagged, pointed teeth where she had any at all, and continual lines of spittle trailing down her whiskered chin, Crawa terrified Aldera. Not simply because of her dark, all-knowing eyes, but because she lived under the hill with her raven charges, eating what they ate, sleeping where they slept, awash in their secrets.

Once, when Aldera had dared to creep in seeking one of the raven women's many texts on healing, she'd glimpsed Crawa crouched on the floor among the ravens, gnashing on the innards of a dead rabbit. Crawa had looked over her shoulder with a feral snarl, dark blood mingled with the spittle on her chin, and then gone back to eating alongside the dark birds.

Aldera had run away, not daring to claim the book. Later, she'd forsaken her pride and begged Pana to retrieve the volume for her, much to her new sister's delight.

"I must go into the temple?" Now, Aldera whispered out of fear, rather than caution. "Right now? At night?" Entering the temple was scary enough during the day.

"Not only go in," Pana said firmly. "You must come out with a feather."

All about Aldera, the other girls nodded.

She swallowed, but the lump of fear crafted pain in her throat would not be dislodged. Her gaze flicked to Talla, then to several other girls who were older. They had all gone in. When her time came, Pana certainly would.

Aldera held out her hand. "Give me a candle."

Pana shook her head. "No. These are tests of bravery. You go in without light, and you go in alone."

Aldera swallowed again, digesting that with fresh fear, for she would not be alone. Somewhere inside the temple, Crawa lurked. Aldera clamped her teeth hard together and nodded. If the Raven Goddess needed proof of her bravery for her to become part of her mother's people, then Aldera would give her proof.

She only wished she weren't so terrified of doing so.

II

The murmured well wishes of her sisters trailing off behind her, Aldera pushed open the rough wooden door. She felt a flash of relief when the hinges issued no creak. The smells of the temple, earth, guano, marsh berry candles, and dried blood, slipped out to wrap about her, making her gag. She cocked her head, holding her breath to listen to the sounds within.

The soft swish of feathers rubbing together came from all sides, and she knew that daylight would reveal ravens perched about the room on the great tree roots that draped the ceiling and wriggled down the walls. The waning moon cast a narrow, pathetic swath of silver light through the doorway, illuminating nothing save the glint of dozens of beady dark eyes.

Assessing eyes, yes, but not angry and, insofar as Aldera could tell, not one pair belonged to Crawa.

Aldera looked over her shoulder, taking in the ring of gray-clad girls gathered in the shimmering moonlight without. She sucked in a deep breath of the crisp, pine-scented air of the village, then turned back to plunge into the darkness under the hill.

The door closed behind her with a dull thud and Aldera started, whirling. Only darkness met her gaze, no matter which way she turned. She had seen no one near the door. Had some power closed her in? A breeze she had not felt? Pana, simply to torment her?

Or was Crawa here in the dark with her even now, waiting?

Realizing she'd turned too many times and lost track of which direction she faced in the darkness, Aldera reached out a tentative hand. Nothing met her seeking fingers. She pivoted slowly, with purpose, her heart pounding so hard that her ears felt stuffed with wool. She couldn't hear the feathers any longer. Only her own ragged breath.

Her fingers brushed against something hard.

She yanked them back, then reached out again. Wood. The rough wood of the door.

Aldera went to that reassuring barrier. Placing her back against it, she waited, working to slow her breathing and hoping her eyes would eventually be able to discern something. Any shape or glint of light.

A slow breath in. An even slower one out. With jittery amusement, she realized she'd learned to do the same when Pana angered her, for she did need the younger girl. No matter how they might disagree, Pana was the one tasked with teaching her, and learning from Pana required forbearance.

That learning also required a great deal of time spent studying the text on her own. In fact, aside from the day with the dead rabbit, Aldera had been inside this temple many times without fleeing. Often, Crawa did not even appear but when she did, uneasy as she made Aldera feel, she had never said or done anything. Merely watched with dark eyes full of knowledge.

For Crawa sent the dark birds far and wide across Cendoria. Her ravens spied out the doings of all, be they farmers, priests, or kings. They reported back to their wizened caretaker, and she to Saderia.

Crawa must know of this trial. If each girl in the village entered the temple before the dawn of their twelfth year, Crawa knew as much. She would even have done so in her youth. Aldera was silly to fear collecting a feather from this place. In fact, they were often gathered for use in bedding, in ornaments, or as quills, and fresh ones were always scattered about the floor. Crawa would not care if she took one any more than the ravens would.

Aldera sucked in a deep breath, mustered her courage and said, "It's Aldera. I am sorry to wake you, but may I have a feather, please? It-it's for this trial. It's my twelfth birthday."

Stone scraped against stone. There came a sharp tap. A wet, metallic smell reached Aldera's nostrils even as she caught sight of a shower of tiny sparks. A little pile of tinder flared to life atop a flat stone.

Aldera swallowed back a yelp of fear as the flame illuminated Crawa squatting on the dirt floor, her face rendered even more ghoulish by the sharp, dancing shadows of the small blaze.

"I-I'm sorry to disturb you," Aldera said again, her words a whisper.

Their shadows large and grotesque against the earth-and-root ceiling, the ravens stirred on their swooping perches. The rustle of their feathers undulated through the space like water lapping on the shore of a lake.

Aldera pressed against the door, the solid wood both reassuring and unsettling. The way out, and yet closing her in. "I only need a feather." And she didn't care if she impressed Pana with a wing feather, or even one from a raven's tail. Aldera would happily take a down feather and leave. "Any feather will do."

The hunched figure before her, her gray garb riddled with holes and hanging loose on a fine-boned frame, dipped her head.

Taking that as permission, Aldera wrenched her gaze from Crawa to study the floor.

There were, indeed, feathers scattered about the shadowy packed dirt. Before her, in fact, a stubby tail feather rested on the temple floor.

The fingertips of one hand still touching the wood of the door out of fear that Crawa would extinguish the flame she'd sparked, Aldera inched forward. She dipped down.

Crawa let out a sound, both hissing and garbled. A drop of spittle sputtered in the small fire she'd sparked.

Aldera froze mid-stoop. Her gaze sought the old woman, fearful and questioning. "Not that feather?"

A raven swooped down, a lovely long black pinion in his beak. He dropped it before Aldera. With a squawk, he launched upward again.

Aldera stared at the feather for a moment, then

looked again to Crawa. "This one?"

Crawa dipped her head.

Moving slowly in case she'd misunderstood, Aldera grasped the feather, then rose. She inched back to the door. "Thank you. I—"

The moment her back touched the door, the flame before Crawa went out, darkness dropping like a cloak.

Aldera drew a quick, startled breath. No sound came from the room before her. "T-thank you," she reiterated.

The words sounded back hollowly.

Feeling completely, utterly alone in the dark under the hill, Aldera yanked open the door and stumbled out into the glow of the winter moon.

"She has it," someone whispered excitedly.

"A perfect pinion," another girl said.

They converged on Aldera, their praise and joy at her success not diminished by the quiet of their voices in the slumbering village. Tension drained from her, replaced by an odd warmth. For the first time since coming to live with her mother's people, Aldera felt as if maybe, perhaps, she might belong there.

"It is a nice feather," Pana said, her tone far cooler than her words. "I'm pleased to see you were able to complete the very easiest of the tasks."

Aldera pulled away from the other girls to face Pana, their leader even if she did have only nine years. "I am ready for the next trial."

"I hope so." Rather than mocking, Pana appeared quite serious as she continued, "And I

hope you are a good swimmer. Come, to the river."
Pivoting, she set out east through the village.

Aldera shivered, awash with fresh worry. She
knew how to swim but the river was ice cold and
swift, and the night dark. She hoped that whatever
they had planned for her, it was not too dangerous.

The other girls massed around her, still
speaking excitedly about what a fine feather she'd
come out with as they set out along the trail to the
river, but Aldera's sureness of moments ago had
fled. Somehow, all the warmness and comradery
their praise had instilled in her had fled at Pana's
mention of a swim.

III

Aldera stood beside the roiling waterway, shivering in her underclothes. Before her the river ran north to south, seeming to carry the moonlight that glittered along the surface ever onward, to eventually spill into the ocean. Aldera had never seen the ocean and standing here, her breath clouding before her in the night, she suddenly feared she never would. At least, not while her spirit remained within her form, for if she failed her body might reach the sea eventually.

"I don't see why you want to get your underthings wet," Pana said where she stood at Aldera's side.

Aldera gave a stubborn shake of her head. In the village where she'd lived, people did not go about unclothed. Not that they did here in the pinewood, either. At least, not often, but the women here seemed to have a far different idea of modesty than those in Aldera's home. "I'm not taking them off."

Pana shrugged. "They're your underthings so I suppose you don't have to, but you'll regret not listening to me." She gestured at the edge of the forest. "We'll have your cloak and your clothes waiting by the fire when you come out."

Indeed, the other girls had already cleared the dusting of snow and thick bed of pine needles from a space beside a pair of large boulders and sparked some tinder. Now, they crouched about the small flame, feeding it twigs.

"You won't find any rocks near the shore," Pana continued, her voice low. "It's all muddy or big stones you can't pry free. You have to get out to the shoal. You can't tell where it is by looking, except at the end of summertime when the water is slow and lower, but it's not far. Just keep swimming until your feet can touch. And try to swim upriver. That will keep you from drifting too far down. You're lucky you weren't born in the spring. I've known two girls who were washed away in spring when the river is fierce, not slow like it is now."

Aldera cast her a horrified look. "Washed away? To...to die?"

Pana shrugged again. "They didn't come back."

"Why are you making me do this?" Aldera asked softly.

"You said you want to stay and learn our ways. How to heal and hide from sight and become a raven and fly." Pana appraised her from the corner of her eye. "No one will truly accept you if you don't do this. Maybe not even our goddess, when it's time for your Ritual of Becoming. Maybe...maybe you won't even be able to work any magic at all, if you don't do this. You have to try, Aldera, or you may as well go home."

Aldera shuddered, but this time not from the cold. Aware that Pana watched her closely, she tried to mask her fear. Aldera had not left her home to the west because she wanted to be a raven woman. She'd left to escape the clutches of a brutal nobleman. Just the thought of his avaricious, lascivious eyes made her want to jump into the river, no matter the risks.

But he would not remain in the village where her family lived forever. He claimed he would stay only until the young duke reached his majority.

That day was over six years hence. Six years was a long time to live in this village and not be accepted as one of these women, but death lasted far, far longer. Aldera worried at her lower lip with her teeth, uncertain if her best choice was the river.

"You are certain you know how to swim?" Pana asked. "I've never seen you do so."

"Because I arrived in the cold of autumn and we have not yet reached spring, let alone summer," Aldera replied, eyeing the dark, moon-dappled water.

"You're only a useless village girl, but I do not want you to die," Pana admitted. Aldera glanced at her in time to see her new sister pull a face and add, "And mother would be very angry with me."

"I can swim. I will make it to the shoal." Because she did want to be one of these women, and she wanted to fly. "I will get a river stone, and come back." At least, Aldera hoped she would.

Pana nodded and turned her back to the river. Raising her voice she said, "Aldera is ready to go in."

"May the goddess know your bravery," the girls answered, as they had before Aldera entered the temple.

Not looking back at them, she strode out into the

river.

Pana was right that the current was not as swift as Aldera had feared, for the river was not yet engorged by spring's thaw, but the water was cold. Colder than anything she'd ever felt. Colder than snow, or even ice. As she went deeper in, up to her neck, she feared the shock of the icy water would still her heart.

She started her limbs moving, her strokes at first awkward and slow, her arms shaking. Soon, she found her rhythm, her mother's lessons echoing in her mind. Fleetingly, she wondered if this was why her mother, Deora, had insisted she learn to swim, a skill not normally taught to children in the village Aldera was from. But then, their mother had taught her brother Kylem as well, and she could not have had any inkling that he would ever come to live with the raven women.

A distant shout caught Aldera's attention. She paused to tread water and her feet found slippery, scummed-over stone. Turning back she could see that Pana and the other girls were pointing downward, urging her to secure a stone. Aldera waved to them, nodding. She'd reached the shoal.

Her feet slipped against the rounded stones below, the current tugging at her. Aldera kept her arms moving, fighting against the flow of water. Did she dare go under? The water was so cold, so dark and fast, she feared she could be carried away and quickly disoriented.

Something slid past Aldera, brushing against her leg. A submerged branch?

"Hurry, before they find you," Pana's voice called, louder than the rest.

"Hurry," the other girls echoed, their hands cupped about their mouths to lend distance to their warning.

Something touched Aldera's leg again, this time going the opposite direction…not with the current.

Aldera peered downward but the water was blacker than night. What swam with her? Pana had issued no warning. Given no advice other than to find the shoal and get a stone.

Her feet almost too numb already to feel the stones beneath them, she tried to wrap her toes about a rock. She yanked her leg up, but the river pulled the rock free before she could grab it. She plunged her foot back downward.

Her sole met something hard and darting, whatever it was speeding away.

Aldera yelped, jumping.

She slipped on the slimy rocks under her feet. Her arms windmilled. With a cry, she went under.

Icy water slammed into her mouth and nose. She got her feet under her, pressing upward. Several hard, muscled bodies slammed into her legs from behind, knocking them back out from under her. Frigid water closed about her head.

More creatures slammed into her. Her arms. Her back. One collided with her head. Aldera fell backward beneath the surface. Long, lithe forms tangled about her feet. Something sharp bit into her leg.

Her hands found the river bottom. Snatching up

a fist-sized rock, she brought it around, blindly slamming it into the snakelike body affixed to her leg.

Writhing, it released her and darted away.

Aldera grabbed a second rock. She swung her arms about, trying to get her feet under her. Flailing madly, she hit more bodies, sending them fleeing. Her lungs, her whole chest, felt ready to explode. She surged to her feet.

Water cascaded from her in rivulets. She sucked in air and swung, then swung again, and again. The rocks she held collided with the creatures swarming about her. Maddened with fear and pain, her legs and arms numbed by the ice-flecked water, she kept swinging until she found nothing to hit.

With a sob, Aldera launched off the shoal, back into deeper water. Something wrapped about her uninjured leg and she kicked with the other, dislodging the long, sinewy creature. Rocks in hand, unwilling to give up the only weapons she had, she floundered into the deeper, faster current. The water swept her numbed form south.

Through the blur of her vision, movement on the shore caught her attention. Pana scrambled along the shoreline through the dead marsh grass, yelling, "Drop the rocks. Forget about the rocks. Swim."

Aldera focused on the shore. She was not far, but she needed to release the rocks to swim well enough to fight against the swiftness of the river. She treaded water bobbing, getting pulled farther south.

Kicking, surging upward, she thrust her torso as far from the river as she could, and hurtled the rocks at Pana. Shock filled her sister's face as they arced out over the water. One plopped down before her, sending up a splash. Where the other went, Aldera didn't see as she doped back down, going under. She surged upward through the water, getting her head free to bob above the surface.

She had to swim.

Fighting the current, fighting the icy numbness in her limbs, she struggled for shore. Her world narrowed to the group of girls scurrying along the bank, calling to her.

Finally, her flailing arms hit mud. She dropped her feet, finding mud there, too. Sobs taking her, Aldera half stumbled, half crawled up the muddy bank. The other girls reached out for her, their hands finding her fingers, her arms, and pulling. They hauled her up onto the dead marsh grass and they all collapsed, gasping.

As the harsh breathing stilled, Talla gasped out, "Why didn't you get a rock quick and leave? The eels almost had you."

Aldera shook her head, her teeth chattering too hard to talk.

"We have to get her back to the fire," Pana said.

"Do you have her rock?" someone asked.

"Right here." Pana sounded pleased. "She's lucky I caught it."

Where she lay at their feet in the brown grass, Aldera struggled to focus on Pana. Her new sister held a fist-sized, rounded rock. Smooth and dark, it also glittered, and Aldera thought a line of quartz might run through the stone.

"It's awful pretty," one of the girls murmured.

"It will please the goddess." Pana sounded as smug as if she'd claimed the stone from the river herself.

Hands helped Aldera up. The arms of her sisters wrapped about her, supporting her as they went back north, where Aldera could see the glow of their fire. She worked to make her feet move, not wanting to stumble and pull over the girls who helped her. Before her, Pana led the way.

Instead of going straight to the fire, Pana insisted on leading Aldera back to the river and cleaning off the mud as best they could, no matter how Aldera tried to protest through her chattering. She was then allowed to stand by the small blaze to dry, warmth slowly returning to her limbs. Once she felt able to move again, Aldera awkwardly tugged on her clothes.

Across the fire from her, Pana tutted. "Your underthings are all brown and dirty. Now you'll need to wash them and your clothes. If you're going to stay here with us, you'll need to learn to listen to me. I told you it would be better to go naked."

Anger surged through Aldera, staving off the last lingering chill that held her tongue. "And yet you did not tell me there are eels out there."

"You didn't tell her about the eels that live on the shoal?" Talla blurted, her eyes wide and filled with reflected firelight.

About the fire, the other girls appeared equally astonished.

Pana shrugged. "I didn't want you to be too scared to go."

"I would not have been," Aldera muttered.

"How was I to know that? Everyone knows village girls are afraid of everything. You are even afraid to take off all your clothes."

Aldera stared at the other girl, uncertain how to explain that modesty was not born of fear. Finally, she shook her head. The night wore on and one trial remained. She did not have time for an argument with Pana.

Taking up her cloak and trying to ignore the line of dampness that her tattered braid made down the center of her back, Aldera said, "What is the final trial?"

Her expression all innocence, Pana replied, "It's simple. You just have to climb a tree."

"Simple?" Aldera repeated. Somehow, she doubted that.

IV

Aldera stood at the base of the massive pine, her rock and feather tucked into her tunic, and stared at the giant, gaping, rotten hole. The trunk, coarse bark glinting like scales by the light of a lowering moon, was as wide around as the dwelling Aldera shared with Pana. A man astride could ride through the sap-dripping, dark edged rend in the tree's base. Where they would be riding too Aldera didn't know, for no light reached past that scarred entrance.

"How did the hole get there?" Aldera asked, awed as she gazed upward at the massive pine, its top lost in the dark of the night sky high above.

"They say a wyvern made it thousands of years ago," Talla replied from where she stood beside Pana. "Ripped the trunk open with his claws, trying to get a raven woman out."

Pana snorted, raising the candle she'd lit from their now extinguished fire by the river. The yellow glow flickered off dark brown rivulets of sap that dripped and pooled like frozen blood. "Which is nonsense. How would a raven woman get in there if there wasn't a hole? And anyhow, there's no such thing as wyverns."

Talla turned an annoyed look on the younger girl. "Why not? We have magic. *His* servants must as well."

"We do not speak of *him*," Pana snapped. "And anyhow, *his* servants aren't smart enough to learn magic."

Aldera realized they must mean the autumn god, Tumpne. Even in her short time with her mother's people, she'd learned that the raven women loathed the autumn god. She knew better than to try to speak of him, but she could not help but ask, "What is a wyvern?"

"It's a great big lizardy thing that flies, and it isn't real." Pana lowered her candle as she spoke, turning to Aldera. Beyond them, well back from the trunk, the other girls formed a nervous semicircle. "You have to go inside, climb up, and put your rock and your feather up there with the others. Then, it will be proven that you're worthy to be one of us."

Aldera eyed the tree again, then her new sister. "That is all?" It was a long way up, presumably in the dark, but there were undoubtedly many hand and foot holes. Aldera thought she could make it.

Pana smirked. "That is all."

A murmur rose from the semicircle of girls.

"That is not all," Talla said with a quick glare at Pana. "The trunk is like a tunnel and it's full of trails made by ants. Once you start up, we'll light them on fire. They'll burn for a while, all the way up, so you'll be able to see, but the ants get pretty angry."

Aldera grimaced. "Will they bite me?"

"They might," Pana admitted. "It doesn't hurt much, unless you're a coward."

Again, Aldera wondered at the younger girl's

strange notions. Much as modesty was not born of fear, being able to endure pain and being brave were not one and the same.

Talla cast Pana a sour look. "How would you know? You've never been in there."

"I know only cowards fail, and that our goddess does not grant her favor to cowards," Pana replied with no hint that Talla's scowl troubled her. Pana turned back to Aldera. "In you go, and then I get to light the fire."

Aldera inched closer to the gaping wound in the hollowed tree. The air looked strangely thick inside. Denser than the darkness alone could explain. "Is that...are those cobwebs?"

Talla nodded. "Yes. The tree is full of spiders. Some of them are very poisonous, but you'll be able to see well enough to avoid those."

Aldera swallowed convulsively. She'd read about the spiders of the Ravenwood in one of the books of lore kept in the temple. The bites of some would kill a grown man in minutes. The green ones, she thought, with the white spot on their back.

Or was it the brown ones with the dark green stripes?

She swallowed down more bile. She would not vomit in front of Pana again, as she'd done her first night in the village.

Turning back to Pana and Talla, Aldera asked, "Is that everything? Trails of fire and angry ants and spiders?" She studied Pana's face as she spoke. "Nothing like the eels? Nothing else hiding in there?" As if angry ants and spiders weren't enough.

Pana raised her gaze heavenward. "Eels don't live in trees, Aldera."

"I said like eels."

"Nothing else," Talla said. "And you truly can do it. The climbing is very easy. Parts of the inside of the tree are left, almost like steps, and there aren't really so many spiders. Only, climb fast. The trails don't burn for very long and you don't want to be in the dark in there."

Aldera nodded. She unclasped her cloak, despite the cold, and handed it to Talla. Aldera didn't want the weight or volume of the flowing gray garment. "I leave the stone and the feather at the top."

Talla nodded. "It's not all the way at the top. You'll see where. There's a ledge and there are loads of them."

Aldera dipped her head again in acknowledgement of that and turned back to the tree. She took a deep breath and, to a renewed chorus of 'May the goddess know your bravery,' she plunged in.

Thick, sticky webs enveloped her, clinging to her hands, her face, her hair. She swept them away, praying no spiders were among them or, worse, already on her.

Shuddering, she forced her attention to the walls of the cavernous interior of the tree.

"Start climbing so I can light the fire," Pana called from without.

Aldera squinted, trying to see in the paltry glow

of moonlight that reached her. She scrubbed her palms over her face in a futile attempt to rub off the remaining cobwebs. Squinting, her eyes growing accustomed to the darkness, she spied undulating protrusions spiraling up one wall. The almost-steps to which Talla had referred.

Though they were set farther apart than normal steps, with gaps of space between them, traversing them still appeared much easier than climbing. Aldera started up, using her hands nearly as much as her feet. Under her palms, the protrusions of wood were oddly ridged, as if the rest of the tree had been scraped away from them with a finely pointed tool.

Light flared below her, accompanied by a sharp, acrid smell, then raced past her up the inside wall of the tree. All about, lines of fire illuminated the living tunnel through which Aldera climbed. The glowing strands formed a delicate, beautiful, almost mesmerizing pattern twining up the inside of the trunk. Aldera stared, feeling as if she could almost comprehend the design. Almost understand the mind that had created such a large, elaborate symbol.

Dark, writhing shapes erupted from the lines of fire, swarming outward.

Aldera started moving again, climbing as quickly as she could.

Pain shot up her leg. She grimaced, looking down, but saw no ants. She rubbed at the leg of her loose gray breeches and the pain intensified. Halting, she yanked up the fabric.

Not an ant but little dots of red forming the outline of a wide bite mark met her seeking gaze, and Aldera recalled the eels. One had latched onto her leg. She'd been so numb and cold by the time she crawled from the river, she'd forgotten.

With a shrug she released the fine gray cloth and resumed climbing. There was nothing to do about the bite now. She must reach the top, and come back down, before the tunnels burned up.

Her leg throbbing more by the moment, she scrambled upward, dodging dense clusters of cobwebs without troubling to identify the spiders within. Pain raced up her leg again, burning like the light decorating the tree-tunnel, and she gasped. Clenching her teeth, she pressed onward.

Dizziness filled her, making the climb more difficult but somewhat dulling the pain creeping up her leg. Aldera blinked, trying to focus on the next step-like protrusion, and the next. She listed to the side. Reaching out, she caught ahold of the inside of the trunk so she wouldn't topple sideways into the open space in the center.

Not fully open, for cobwebs filled and crossed it. Cobwebs like the one into which she'd just stuck her hand, she realized. Stilling, she tried to focus her swaying vision on the hole into which she'd jammed her fingers. A small, brown, green striped spider crawled out onto the back of her hand.

Aldera gulped, sweat trickling down her forehead. The spider didn't move. Merely waited on her exposed, icy skin.

A blur of feathers swept past her vision. A

raven, swooping at her.

Aldera jerked back, afraid the raven would collide with her head.

The raven swooped past her hand, then winged upward, gone, as was the spider.

Aldera jerked her hand back, shaking it, but no sign of the arachnid remained. With a deep breath, her stab of fear having cleared her mind somewhat, she hurried onward.

Ants began to spill onto the steps. Most ignored her, but some nipped at fingers she was forced to place among them. Their little mandibles tore at her skin, but were nothing to the pain consuming her leg. Spiders crept from their dens, farther out into their webs, their spindly legs and venom filled fangs gathering ants as they sought to take advantage of the unexpected bounty. Still Aldera climbed onward.

Her breath came in short gasps, more from pain than exertion, though sweat bathed her brow. A writhing glob of ants dropped down, colliding with her back. A spasm of revulsion rattled her, threatening her shaky stability. She gritted her teeth harder and fought to ignore them as they spread outward, down her clothing and up into her hair.

Finally, panting, she reached a large shelf of living wood. It extended out through a hole in the pine and Aldera pulled herself up, sucking in the cool night air. Weak moonlight spilled in to illuminate piles of stones weighing down glossy black feathers, side by side in matched sets.

Her vision was doubled, she realized, squeezing

her eyes closed. With a shaky hand, she pulled forth the rock she'd brought from the river, clutching it. She pried her lids open and set the rock on the ledger. Her trembling fingers scrambled for the feather.

And fumbled, the pinion slipping free.

Aldera cried out, reaching out as it wafted downward. An ant dropped from her finger, following the feather into a large web several feet below her.

She inched downward, so dizzy now that she feared she might topple sideways off the steps to join the feather her fingers struggled to reach. Only, the spider web wouldn't support her.

The tips of her fingers touched the end of the feather, but she couldn't grasp it. Digging into the web, she pulled, drawing the feather closer. Just as she grabbed the pinion, a large black spider scuttled out to see what disturbed her web. Aldera lurched back, taking the feather with her.

She scrambled back up and slapped the feather down, then set the rock atop. Triumph surged through her.

Going down was more difficult than going up had been. She slipped often, barely catching herself back from plummeting. Ants swarmed the steps now, spiders among them, waging a battle in which Aldera couldn't predict the winner. The spiders were more deadly, but the ants more numerous. She tried to avoid the former as much as she could as she slithered downward but her dizziness and the rapidly dimming lines of light made doing so difficult. She could only hope that none of them stung her. She didn't even know, with the pain in her leg and the bites of the ants, if she would feel a spider's sting.

She hit the bottom with a clatter and scrambled out on her hands and knees, uncertain she could stand. The ring of girls rushed forward, Pana at their center. Talla and another girl reached Aldera first, though, working together to hoist her to her feet.

"Did you do it?" Pana asked, coming to a halt before her.

Aldera nodded, sagging in the grip of the other two girls. "I did."

A grin split Pana's face. "I knew you could do it. I knew you were meant to be one of us. If we hurry, we can make it back in time to celebrate before anyone wakes up. I'm so proud of you."

To Aldera's shock, Pana threw her arms about her in a fierce hug.

Then pulled away, frowning. "You're on fire. Did a spider bite you?"

Aldera shook her head. "I don't know. I don't think so. My leg." She struggled, trying to rally the words that would tell Pana and the others what was wrong, but they wouldn't come to her.

"Your leg?" Pana dropped down and yanked up both of Aldera's trouser legs. She let out a gasp, surging to her feet. "Is that an eel bite?"

Aldera nodded. At least, she tried to. The world bobbed and spun with the attempt.

"Quick, bring me her cloak," Pana called, her

voice loud and far away. "We need two stout branches. We'll get her on a stretcher and carry her back."

Stretcher? Carry her?

Aldera tried to pull away from the arms holding her up, to show Pana that she could walk. She toppled over.

V

Aldera stood in a snow filled valley, the steep walls to either side draped in frozen waterfalls that glittered with breathtaking beauty in the bright afternoon sun. She raised a hand to shield her eyes against the brilliance and turned in a slow circle to take in her surroundings.

Set into the wall at one end of the valley stood a stone arch, engraved with symbols in the raven tongue and topped by two carvings of the dark birds, their beaks nearly touching, their gazes locked for eternity. She couldn't quite make out the symbols from where she stood, and wasn't certain she knew them all. Some were familiar from her studies with Pana, but others were not.

Another turn brought her around to face the other end of the valley, filled by a gathering of low huts such as made up the raven village. Smoke wended upward from warming fires and, even at a distance, Aldera could see the cheerful domesticity. Dark haired women hung wash in the bright winter sun, or sat about a fire weaving. On the nearly still air, she caught the scent of woodsmoke and savory porridge and her mouth watered.

She raised her gaze to look beyond the village, where something shimmered in the sky. Filled, in fact, the far end of the valley. A sort of translucent nothingness, like the wavering of heat unseen above a fire. And beyond that veil of transparent light…Aldera squinted. A tower?

Movement caught her eye. A white robed woman coming down the valley through the snow, her stride so graceful, she seemed hardly to move as she drew closer and yet remained far away, all at once. Her hair flowed outward about her, black as midnight and star-studded, yet no breeze stirred. Her face, cold, calm, beautiful, filled Aldera's mind and yet would not remain there for her to be able to describe it.

Then the woman stood before her and Aldera looked down, aware that she was not worthy to gaze upon that visage.

"You cannot be here," the woman said, her voice like honey spilling down boulders. More firmly, she declared, "You are not here."

Taking in her boot clad feet, Aldera realized she could see through them to snow in which her soles left no impressions. Her legs, too, were faded, insubstantial. She held out a hand, looking through the outline of her fingers.

"Your Saderia was right to call my aid. You have much to do, daughter of Deora."

Aldera's head snapped up at the sound of her mother's name, only to find darkness.

VI

Darkness filled Aldera's senses. Her vision, her mind. Around her, before her, blotting out the world.

Then came the pain. Harsh heat scaled up her leg, sinking her into a different blackness, that of unconsciousness.

Slowly, a buzzing filled her ears. Sensation returned to her limbs. She was warm. Blanket wrapped. The smell of marsh berries and sweet grass wafted about her.

"...told you to give her time," Saderia's voice was saying somewhere above Aldera. Hard and clipped with anger, the words consolidated, further pushing the clinging darkness from her mind. "She was not ready. She knew too little."

"But today is her twelfth birthday. She had to do it." Pana's voice held a whining note. "I don't know why you're so angry with me. All the girls went."

"I know whose idea it was. I know you are their leader."

"Me? I'm only nine. Talla was there. She's thirteen. She already went through the three trials."

"So you are not the leader of your sisters?" Saderia asked, disbelief coloring her voice.

"I will be," Pana muttered. "When you are gone, I will be Saderia."

"Being Saderia is less about giving orders than taking responsibility," Saderia returned harshly.

Aldera could all but feel Pana flinch back from her mother's words.

"And the question is not if you are guilty but in what way you should be punished," Saderia continued.

Punished? Aldera knew Pana had behaved rashly, as she often did, but this time she'd been right. Aldera needed to do what the others did. She wanted to be accepted. By her mother's kin, and by their goddess.

She blinked her eyes open, a blur of memory rattling in her brain. A shadowy vision of white snow and blue winter sky came to her, but it slipped away again, lost. "I wanted to do it," she said. Her voice came out cracked and brittle, and she coughed. Her throat felt choked by cobwebs.

Aldera flinched, hoping it truly wasn't. Had she inhaled them?

"Aldera." Saderia dropped to sit on the edge of the bed, a hand reaching out to press against Aldera's brow, cool and comforting. "How do you feel? How is your leg?"

"My leg?" The eel. "Better, I think."

Saderia smiled. "The goddess saw fit to grant you healing. We are fortunate."

"Because I have much to do?" The words came from Aldera's mouth unbidden, and dizziness stirred through her. She knew not why she'd said them.

Saderia's eyes narrowed but her smile remained

in place. "Certainly you have much to do, but only once you feel able. The eels in the shoal are quite toxic. You should have been warned not to linger there."

"Much to do? She doesn't even know how to do anything yet," Pana groused, flopping down on her bed, across from Aldera's.

"And you," Saderia said, her hand leaving Aldera's forehead. She swiveled to regard Pana. "I can hardly think of a punishment harsh enough. Aldera's mother entrusted her to us. She has been among us for less than two seasons and we nearly lost her."

Aldera struggled to sit up, wanting to appear well. "But I am not lost and I wanted to endure the trials. It isn't Pana's fault. I could have refused."

"You see?" Pana said eagerly. "It's not my fault. It's Aldera's. She wanted to do it."

Saderia turned back to watch Aldera speculatively. "This is what you would have me think? That Pana should know no punishment for her actions because you wished to undergo the trials?"

Aldera nodded. "I did, Saderia. I want to be like the others. I want to be a raven woman."

Saderia's gaze softened and Aldera thought maybe she understood what went unsaid; that Aldera wanted to be accepted. Needed to be. Punishing Pana, or any of the girls, would take away from that.

Besides, what Aldera said was true. She could have refused to undertake the trials.

Saderia stood. "Very well. If you are certain that you take responsibility for this near calamity, I will not gainsay you." She smoothed the front of her black robe, not a white one, and another strange inkling of memory sped through Aldera, but she couldn't cling to the thought as Saderia continued, "Today we celebrate your birth, but tomorrow and every day for ten days, you will rise before dawn to assist with our morning meal. You will not be tardy, or sullen in your work. You will accept your punishment and learn, both our ways and not to behave so foolishly in the future."

Aldera bowed her head. "Yes, Saderia."

"Very well. When you are ready, come outside. The others are waiting for you." With silent grace she strode from their rounded dwelling.

Pana let out an explosive breath. "That was a near thing. I hate having to help with breakfast. You're going to hate it too. You have to be up so early and it's so boring. Just carrying water and heating water and stirring and stirring. Ug. It's the worst."

"It is something I must learn to do eventually." Aldera felt certain all the other girls knew how to make the rich, savory porridge they ate for breakfast in the village. "Porridge?" She could almost recall something. Something important.

"Uh, yes, porridge. You've had it every morning since you got here." Pana leaned forward to study Aldera. "Did you hit your head too, while you were in the river?"

Aldera blinked at Pana, the remnants of

memory scattering. She shook her head, uncertain why she'd even wanted to catch some stray thought or another. What thought would it even be?

"Why are you staring at nothing like that and shaking your head? Is there water in your ears? That's the worst. Way worse than your eel bite, I bet, because the goddess granted Mother healing for that, but you'll have to live with water in your ears until it gets better."

Pana's babbling reminding her, Aldera swung free of her blankets, wanting to see her leg. She was surprised to see she still wore her muddy underthings. Now she would need to clean her clothing and her blankets. Maybe Pana had been right about swimming naked.

Faint pink marks dotted Aldera's leg. She reached down to touch them. They didn't hurt at all.

"Mother says you probably won't even have a scar," Pana supplied, hopping out of her bed. "I'll get your clean clothes so we can go outside. We've missed breakfast but I bet they saved something because it's your birthday."

With that, she went to the end of Aldera's bed and threw open the chest there. Aldera suppressed a cry of annoyance. She didn't have anything Pana couldn't see, but even her own mother wouldn't so cavalierly go through her possessions as Pana did.

Pana pulled out clean underthings and clothes, and even poured water from the pitcher they kept into the washbasin. Shoving a towel at Aldera, she reiterated the order to hurry.

Aldera washed up, realizing she felt very hungry along with being lightheaded. Then she dressed and followed Pana out.

The other girls rushed forward, gathering around Aldera. They hugged her, a sea of voices wishing her joy on her birthday. Many of them squeezed her hand, whispering that she'd been very brave.

"Brave and lucky," one girl piped up.

"Lucky?" Pana snorted. "Her only luck was that I caught one of those rocks she threw at me. After that, she nearly died."

"But she did not," Talla said slowly. "And she is lucky. She was born under the winter moon."

Pana shook her head. "The final moon of winter. The waning moon. That's the worst one."

"That's still the winter moon," the first girl declared.

"Which is much better than any other, especially an autumn one," Talla added with enough smugness aimed at Pana that Aldera could guess under what moon her new sister had been born.

"At least I wasn't born ugly," Pana snapped and stomped away.

"I cannot believe you climbed all that way with an eel bite," one of the girls said, and conversation returned to congratulating Aldera.

Some of the women came over next, wishing her a joyous birthday. They did not mention the girls' trials, but Aldera suspected from the gleam in their eyes and the number of rocks piled on the shelf of living wood high up in the tree that young raven women had been undergoing the unofficial right of passage for years and years. She also thought that perhaps the older women, too, were now more accepting of her.

She basked in the camaraderie of the other girls for the remainder of the morning. Finally, after nearly the whole of autumn and winter, she felt as if she might belong. As if she could be one of these women. Learn their ways and their magic, and someday fly through the trees as a raven. That dream, that hope, at last seemed real, and for an hour or so, Aldera didn't even miss her home and her family.

She spent the afternoon laundering her bedding and clothes, and learning about her morning chores. Helping with breakfast for the village didn't sound difficult but Aldera concluded that, for once, Pana might be right about it being boring. Still, Aldera was determined that she would arrive on time and do well. She had all but asked to be punished, and she would bear her punishment with equanimity.

Finally, the day wound down. Aldera took her evening meal, a rich thick stew that reminded her of her mother's cooking, and slipped away to sit on a stump at the edge of the cluster of rounded huts that made up the raven village. Tired now, she longed for quiet and solitude. She wished her mother could be with her, not far away in the farmhouse where Aldera was raised. Not that she wanted her father and Kylem to lose Deora, but

Aldera needed her mother too.

Sighing, she stirred her stew, her appetite deserting her.

"You did well today, Aldera, daughter of Deora," Saderia's rich contralto said behind her.

Aldera twisted, turning on her makeshift stool to take in the leader of the raven women. "Thank you, Saderia."

"And you were brave to complete the trials."

"Thank you, Saderia," Aldera repeated, flushing.

"But you were also foolish. You had no knowledge of the river. Have had little time to learn of the spiders that dwell in the pines. Could not yet know how Crawa would react to an invasion of her domain."

Aldera looked down, chastened, though she did know the last. Scary as she was, Crawa would not have harmed her. "I wanted…I want to be like the other girls."

"Child, that will never be. If you look inside yourself, I think you know this."

Aldera's head jerked up. Tears pressed against the backs of her eyes. "Why?"

"I do not yet know." Saderia strode closer, her gaze intent as she studied Aldera. "I have my suspicions, but they are only such."

Aldera blinked, then swiped at her eyes with her free hand. "I don't want to be different."

Saderia smiled. "No? I am different, for there is but one Saderia at a time, you know. You would not want to be like me?"

Aldera floundered, for in truth she would not. She did not want to lead. She simply wanted to be. She did not mind being bored. After all, for the village to prosper, someone must stir the porridge. "Pana is the one to be like you."

Saderia produced a handkerchief, the white square stark against her black robe even in the rosy evening light. Rather than offer it, she cupped Aldera's chin lightly and lifted it so she could apply the handkerchief to her cheeks. "I had assumed so. We all have, for Pana has been precocious since birth. Yet today, who took responsibility? Who shouldered blame and offered recompense?" Saderia lowered the handkerchief but didn't release Aldera's chin, studying her face.

Her cheeks heating, for she had not meant to put herself forward, Aldera managed, "I did."

"Yes. You did." Saderia released her and straightened. "You may not wish to be special, child, but you are. I hope you can make peace with that before Cendoria needs you." With that, she turned and walked away, disappearing into the towering pines.

Aldera's shoulders slumped, tension draining from her. She shook her head. As much respect as she held for the leader of the raven women, Saderia was wrong. Aldera was normal. Today, she'd only done what was right, for she had been foolish to let Pana push her into such danger. Aldera deserved the punishment she'd been given.

And to think Cendoria would ever need her, a normal village girl who'd fled to the far corner of the kingdom to live with a group of women feared by most as witches, that was simply nonsensical. Were she the sort that her kingdom would someday rely upon, she would not have fled. She would have found a way to stay and fight off such unwanted attentions. Pana would have.

That decided, Aldera ate her stew and sought her bed, knowing she must be up early the next morning.

She'd just drifted off when Pana came in, her footfalls overloud in a way that Aldera had come to realize was Pana filled with anger. Through her closed lids, Aldera could see the flicker of light. She hoped Pana didn't have a fresh set of trials for her.

Pana clanked a candleholder down on the little table that stood between their beds and plunked down on the side of hers. "Are you asleep?"

Suppressing a sigh that would only aggravate Pana further, Aldera opened her eyes. "Not yet."

"I'm angry with you."

Aldera studied the other girl's pinched face for a moment. "Why? I thought you were happy that I passed the trials and can stay here and be accepted by the winter goddess."

Her arms folded across her chest, Pana pursed her lips for a moment, then said, "I am but you got me into trouble, getting hurt like that."

Aldera opened her mouth, thought better of her first words, and closed it again.

"You cannot deny that you got me in trouble," Pana snapped.

"But I made certain you didn't get punished," Aldera ventured.

Pana glared at her. "Which only made my mother like you more. She said that thing about responsibility and then you were all responsible. Don't think I don't know you did that on purpose."

Tiredness washed over Aldera. She'd been awake for most of the previous night and all of the day, except from when she'd collapsed outside the hollow pine until she'd awoken in her bed. She wanted to go to sleep, not to have a pointless argument with Pana. "You got me back here," she said, seizing on what Pana had done right. "You had the other girls make a litter and carry me back." Aldera didn't know precisely who had done the carrying, but she knew it had happened. "And you caught the stone I threw to you. I'll tell your mother that. I'm sure the other girls have told her, too."

Pana brightened, her arms falling to her sides. "I did get you back to be healed. I gave the right orders at the right time and I didn't panic one bit."

Aldera relaxed against her pillow, relieved she'd be able to sleep without a fight. "Precisely. Like a leader."

Pana's eyes narrowed. "You aren't trying to become Saderia instead of me?"

Aldera stared at her in shock. "I wasn't even born here. I can't be Saderia."

"There isn't a rule like that. I asked Crawa."

Aldera stifled a laugh, one knew she would come out slightly manic. Of course Pana had checked. "I swear to you, I do not want to be

Saderia." She only wanted to live in peace, here with these women until the danger posed by that horrible nobleman was gone from her home.

And until she learned how to become a raven and soar among the pines, not climb up their hollowed out, ant and spider-filled centers.

"And I caught the rock," Pana added, flopping back on her bed. "If I hadn't, you couldn't have passed the trials, so you owe me. You would have failed without me, and then died in the forest from your eel bite."

Aldera kept silent, having no answer to that which wouldn't lead to a fight.

"And so long as you don't want to be Saderia, we can be friends and I'll keep teaching you."

"Thank you," Aldera murmured, settling deeper into her cozy sheets. They smelled of sunshine and pine smoke, because she'd had to place them near the great fire in the center of the village to get them dry.

A contented sigh left her as she recalled her sense of belonging that morning. No, she had no desire to be Saderia. Let Pana have that honor, and responsibility. All Aldera wanted was to be like the other girls. To not be the different, strange one among them. She did not need to lead, and she certainly did not want the responsibility of ever being needed by all of Cendoria.

DAUGHTERS OF
AWEN

PREVIEW

I

Gowned in gray, Aldera trailed her mother and little brother down the dusty road and into the village. As they trudged along the wide central lane, other mourners spilled from buildings and side streets until Aldera became stifled among the press of adults, struggling to stay within sight of her mother's dark locks. Finally, in a bleak sooty wave, they all flowed from the village and over the rim of the valley that sheltered the cemetery. Everyone had turned out to bid farewell to the old duke.

As they passed through the gate at the mouth of the cemetery, her mother turned aside, leading Aldera and her brother, Kylem, to where a group of children clustered under the sweeping branches of an ancient maple. Rows of graves curved away before them, following the slope of the valley wall. On the path, a long serpentine line of mourners wove between mounded sepulchers, reaching from the cemetery's gate to the old duke's family well.

"Stay here with the other children," Mother said, placing Kylem's hand in Aldera's before rejoining the line of adults.

At eleven, Aldera hadn't seen many funerals, but she knew children weren't expected to go forward and look down into the deep well where a person's ancestors awaited them. Not unless they were related to the deceased. Aldera wasn't related to the dead duke and she didn't want to look. The duke's family was old, their well layered generations deep. She shuddered at the thought of all those bones.

Only nine, her little brother Kylem peered about, his expression eager. He didn't sense the pall that had fallen over their parents at the death of the old duke. Took no note of the tension about their mouths. Didn't lie awake at night listening to them argue in voices too low to reveal anything but strain.

Kylem tried to tug free and Aldera squeezed his hand tight, not wanting him to run off, down onto the valley floor where children were not to go. She knew he sought their father. Their father, along with three other knights, would bear the litter holding the duke's body. Kylem loved to see Father in his armor.

As the last of the mourners straggled in, a pewter-robed priest of Deyja, god of the dead, emerged from the little domed chapel at the back of the cemetery. Looking past that building, Aldera took in the craggy peaks of the Keng Range, ringed with dingy clouds, before more movement caught her eye. The duke's litter hoisted between them, her father and the other knights marched from the chapel. In slow procession, they bore the old duke on his final earthly journey.

The priest moved to stand beside the thick stone lid as the knights reached the duke's family well. In silence, they used ropes to lower the shrouded body to join its ancestors in the ground's somber embrace. Cold air from the watching mountains crawled across the ground to follow the old duke down into his grave.

Aldera, her sorrow mingling with that of the villagers, watched as her father and the other knights moved back to make way for the priest. He sprinkled salt into the gaping hole, his round face serious with the importance of his duty. Deepening his voice, he called on Deyja to accept this new addition to the realm of the afterlife. Behind him, the clouds shrouding the Keng Range darkened, but inside the cemetery, the morning sun shone bright, highlighting tears with glittering brilliance.

Aldera and Kylem remained where their mother had left them as the throng of villagers shuffled past the duke's family well, looking down into the pit to bid farewell to a fair ruler. Many followed their words with a copper coin and a wish for the dead duke to carry to the gods. Aldera didn't have a coin to give, or a wish strong enough to draw her so near the dead. She was sure Kylem would wish to grow up to be a great knight like their father, but he had no coin either. What their mother whispered to the dead duke as she leaned low over the gaping hole, Aldera didn't know.

Above where she and Kylem stood, autumn leaves blazed, lit like torches by the sun to stand in bright contrast to the inky clouds churning around the mountains. Aldera's wandering gaze caught on thin lines of smoke, marking the far-off Temple of Deyja where it nestled into the feet of the Keng Range. Their youthful priest came from there, as did all servants of Deyja. Lonely men who took the long path into the mountains to offer their service to the god of the dead. They spent years training in the dark stone temple before being dispersed across the land to aid the souls of those seeking passage into the after realm.

A new flicker of movement snagged Aldera's attention. Her breath caught. A raven, winging in from the east.

In a harsh voice, the bird called out, sending a murmur of disquiet through the throng of mourners. Many made signs to ward off evil as the raven dipped low. With a grating shriek, the dark bird dropped a gleaming gold coin into the old duke's family well. Deep in the earth, the coin landed with a thump as the raven winged away to the west.

The villagers pulled back in superstitious fear, although not all had said their goodbyes. Uncertainty on his face, the priest concluded the ceremony, his words rapid now. When he finished, Aldera's father and the other knights lifted the heavy stone lid. Muscles straining, they capped the duke's family well.

Like many of her father's generation, war had kept the old duke from producing an heir until late in life. He left behind only his nine-year old son, Lord Thaler, who choked back tears as he managed the traditional words of goodbye. The priest of Deyja stood to one side of the young duke in silent solidarity. At Thaler's other shoulder loomed his newly declared guardian, Norstum, a duke of the

Western Realm who happened to be visiting when the old duke died.

Aldera knew Norstum by reputation, for he was the only surviving cousin to the king. He was famous for his mother's refusal to marry his father, even though they were well-known lovers. In spite of Norstum's ties to the crown, everyone called him the bastard duke and, while she didn't know the details of why, she knew most felt he deserved all connotations of the name.

Behind their graces Thaler and Norstum, the bastard duke's newest wife lingered like one of the graveyard's apparitions. A slip of a girl, her voluminous gray mourning cloak and constant look of fear reduced her to little more than a pair of wide blue eyes.

When Lord Thaler finished speaking, the other children streamed down the hill like a rush of water released by a dam's break. The villagers hurried in the direction of the chapel, as eager as their children to get the service over on a market day, but Aldera's parents turned up the path between the graves. As a knight, their father stood a step above the peasantry and their family rarely joined the villagers in their religious observances. When their parents drew near, Father reached out an arm, gesturing Aldera and Kylem to join them.

"Sir Onurrun." Turning at the sound of her father's name, Aldera sighted Norstum across a row of graves, his wife lagging behind him. "A word."

"Yes, Your Grace?" Her father strode back

deeper into the valley, placing his body between the bastard duke and his family.

Aldera felt her mother's arm wrap about her shoulders. When he would have followed their father, Mother caught Kylem to her other side.

Norstum came forward to meet Aldera's father on the narrow path, the bottom of his heavy fur cloak gathering dead leaves with every step. "It occurs to me it is fortuitous I happen to be here."

"Does it?" her father asked in a voice notably devoid of warmth.

The bastard duke gestured over his shoulder to Lord Thaler, who stood crying before his family's well. "Aye, it does. Why, that boy is not yet fit to rule, and there are none nearby with sufficient rank to school him. In fact, no others of noble blood survive in his line. The ravages of war, I should say."

He paused, but her father issued no sound, neither agreeing nor denying.

Norstum held his silence a moment longer, then said, "I know some might suggest you for his guardian, but even though the ignoble rabble in these parts regard you as a hero of sorts, it would hardly be fitting for a knight to rear a duke, don't you agree? It would be tantamount to disaster. The Truth knows what would have transpired in this dukedom if I weren't by chance here to take matters in hand."

Again, the duke fell silent. He met her father's eyes with easy unconcern. Lost somewhere in the gold and red leaves of the maple, a lark trilled.

"Isn't that right, Onurrun?" Norstum finally pressed.

"Yes, Your Grace."

With a satisfied nod, the duke continued, "Which is why we must all thank Tumpne that here I am." Norstum's gaze slid past Aldera's father to rest on her, where she huddled to her dam. "And it appears I must stay here for some time, being in charge, as it were. But my poor Daisey has no suitable women about. It's customary to provide a visiting noblewoman with a native to the region. Someone to help her feel at home."

After another strained silence, Aldera's father murmured, "Yes, Your Grace."

"I think your daughter would do nicely," Norstum said. A chill ran through Aldera. Her mother's arm squeezed tighter about her. "I'd like to have your daughter at the castle. For my Daisey."

Aldera pulled her gaze from the duke's face, repulsed by his slightly open mouth, the voracious glint in his eyes. The way his nostrils flared as if he meant to fight. Would she really have to go to the castle and live with him?

"I will have your daughter for my Daisey's lady," Norstum reiterated, his light tone slipping. "In three days' time, she will move to the castle."

"Yes, Your Grace," her father said, bowing low. He turned as he rose, using widespread arms to usher his family before him along the path. Aldera wanted to protest, but a glance at her mother's anger-infused face stilled her tongue. Trembling in every limb, Aldera could feel the bastard duke's gaze on them until they crested the valley's rim and passed from view.

She kept her focus on the leaf-strewn roadway as they hurried home. Normally, she would have stooped to collect the prettiest leaves, but her mother's tight grip, and the covetous look in Norstum's eyes, filled Aldera with fear. Even Kylem was quiet as hasty steps carried them home.

Aldera's mother rounded on her father as soon as the door of their tidy farmhouse closed. "You cannot mean to let that man take Aldera."

"I have no such intention. Be easy, Deora."

"Then what will we do?" her mother said, her voice choked.

Aldera and Kylem stood just inside the door. She looked at her little brother, finding his eyes as wide and fearful as she knew her own must be.

"We'll send her away." Aldera's father drew her mother to him, cupping her head against his broad chest. "To your people."

Her mother pulled back, worry etching deep lines into her face as she contemplated Aldera.

"It's the only place he'll not dare send for her," her father said, answering arguments her mother hadn't yet spoken.

"Why can't Aldera go to the duke's castle and stay near?" Kylem whispered. He wrapped his arms around Aldera's waist.

She hugged Kylem, watching her parents. "To Mother's people?" Her mother said little of the village where she grew up, but Aldera knew everyone feared the women who lived there…the raven women. Even though her mother had not been there in years, some of the villagers still feared her, as well. Often enough, behind her mother's back, Aldera saw them make signs against evil.

Her mind went back to the raven at the funeral. How odd for it to come, and to drop a coin. Everyone had flinched back from the large ragged-winged bird. Everyone but her mother.

"My sisters will take you in. You will be safe with them." Aldera's mother smiled down at her, but there was no smile in her eyes.

"Aldera can't go," Kylem said.

Aldera squeezed her brother tighter. She was afraid to leave, afraid to go to the mysterious raven village, but her fear of Norstum was greater. "How will I get there?"

She'd never ventured more than a few hours' walk into the woods and never alone. She knew her mother's people were somewhere away to the east. Even riding, it would take days to reach them. Three sets of eyes turned to her father for an answer.

"Braan will take you," he said. "You will leave tonight."

"Onurrun." Her mother's voice was high.

"She must leave tonight." Hands on her mother's shoulders, he argued with his eyes. "Norstum is no fool."

A dizzy haze enveloped Aldera as her mother took her arm and dragged her up the steep farmhouse stairs. In something near rage, her mother pillaged Aldera's wardrobe and trunk, clothes flying about. The frenzy lasted only moments before she grabbed Aldera by the arm again and hurtled back down the steps, clutching a large canvas sack.

They tried to eat their midday meal, but her mother kept hiding her face behind her apron. The few bites Aldera took seemed to lurch around in her gut as though they might come back out. Kylem pushed his food about, nibbling on bread, his gaze never leaving Aldera's face. Her father ate his stew slowly. Having served the old duke in many a battle, he alone was accustomed to eating under such strain.

When their meal was done, her father readied the cart to take to town, as he often did on market day. Aldera was to hide in the back until the crowd died down. Avoiding the prying eyes of the village, she would slip onto Braan's wagon with a message to give him. A message telling him to take her away.

I hope you enjoyed this peek at Aldera's journey. To read more, and to learn the fate of all Cendoria, get your copy of *Daughters of Awen* today.

www.books2read.com/DaughtersofAwen

ABOUT the AUTHOR

Summer Hanford is an author of Epic Fantasy, Swashbuckling Historical Fiction, Sweet Regency Romance, and Pride and Prejudice retellings, and writes her Fantasy Novels under Summer H Hanford. She lives in the Finger Lakes region of New York with her husband and compulsory, deliberately spoiled, cat. The newest addition to their household, an energetic setter-shepherd mix, is still not yet appreciated by the cat, even after six years, but in true dog form, he'll never stop trying, and he is well loved by the humans.

Since the moment she read her first novel, Summer's passion has always been writing. As a child growing up on a dairy farm, she built castles made of hay and wielded swords made of fence posts. She is also passionate about animals, travel, and organizing her closet. Nothing pleases her more than a row of tops broken down by sleeve length and ordered by color…except working on her latest novel with her cat in her lap, her dog lounging on the rug dreaming of squirrels, and a cup of tea at hand.

For more about Summer, visit:
www.summerhanford.com

Made in the USA
Columbia, SC
04 October 2024